Let's Eat
Lunch

Clare Hibbert

Cherrytree books are distributed in the United States by
Black Rabbit Books, P.O. Box 3263, Mankato, MN, 56002

Printed in China by WKT Company Ltd.

Library of Congress Cataloging-in-Publication Data
Hibbert, Clare, 1970-
   Let's eat lunch / Clare Hibbert. -- 1st ed.
      p. cm. -- (Sparklers)
   Originally published: London : Evans Brothers Ltd., 2007.
   Includes index.
   Summary: "Covers a range of healthy lunches from around the
world and how the foods people eat may change with the seasons.
Includes simple recipe"--Provided by publisher.
   ISBN-13: 978-1-84234-528-3
   ISBN-10: 1-84234-528-1
   1. Luncheons--Juvenile literature. I. Title. II. Series.

TX735.H53 2009
641.5'3--dc22

                                                 2007046382

First edition
9 8 7 6 5 4 3 2 1

First published in 2007 by Evans Brothers Ltd.
2A Portman Mansions, Chiltern Street, London W1U 6NR, United Kingdom

Produced for Evans Brothers Limited by
White-Thomson Publishing Ltd.

Copyright © Evans Brothers Limited 2007
Educational consultant: Sue Palmer MEd FRSA FEA
Project manager: Clare Hibbert
Picture research: Amy Sparks
Design: Balley Design Limited
Creative director: Simon Balley
Designer/Illustrator: Michelle Tilly

Contents

Lunchtime

crrr—unch!

This book is about lunch.

What time do **you** eat your lunch?

5

Eating Together

Do you **eat** your lunch at school?

Who do you sit with?

chatter!

chatter!

When do you eat lunch
with your family?

11

Hot and Cold

blow

Soup warms you up on a cold day.

Lunch Outside

Lunch in Australia

sizzle

Barbecues are for cooking food outside.

Lunch in China

This woman sells dumplings.

Something Sweet

Tasty!

Do you eat fruit after lunch?

apple tree

Can you think of any fruits that grow on trees?

Lunchtime Drinks

splash!

What do you drink with lunch?

slurp

smoothie

Milkshakes and smoothies taste good!

19

Make It: Greek Salad

Mix these things together to make a Greek salad.

feta cheese ✓
cucumber ✓
tomato ✓
olives ✓
yellow pepper ✓
olive oil ✓
lemon juice ✓

Eat it with tasty pita bread.

21

Notes for Adults

Sparklers books are designed to support and extend the learning of young children. The books' high-interest subjects broaden young readers' knowledge and interests, making them ideal teaching tools as well.

Themed titles
Let's Eat Lunch is one of four **Food We Eat** titles that explore food and meals from around the world. The other titles are:
Let's Eat Breakfast   Let's Eat Dinner   Celebration Food

Areas of learning
Each **Food We Eat** title introduces educational concepts (such as personal development, literacy and mathematical skills) with subtlety and care. Children increase their knowledge and understanding of the world while developing their creativity.

Reading together
When sharing this book with younger children, take time to explore the pictures together. Encourage children by asking them to find, identify, count or describe different objects. Point out different colors or textures.

Allow quiet spaces in your reading so that children can ask questions or repeat your words. Try pausing mid-sentence so children can predict the next word. This sort of participation develops early reading skills.

Follow the words with your finger as you read them aloud. The main text is in Infant Sassoon, a clear, friendly font specially designed for children learning to read and write. The labels and sound effects on the pages add fun, engage the reader, and give children the opportunity to distinguish between different levels of communication. Where appropriate, labels, sound effects, or main text may be presented in phonic spelling. Encourage children to imitate the sounds.

As you read the book, you can also take the opportunity to talk about the book itself with appropriate vocabulary, such as "page," "cover," "back," "front," "photograph," "label," and "page number."

You can also extend children's learning by using the books as a springboard for discussion and further activities. There are a few suggestions on the facing page.

Pages 4–5: Lunchtime

Encourage children to keep a food diary, either as a group or individually. Divide a big piece of paper into seven sections, one for each day of the week. Each afternoon, encourage children to draw, paint, or stick photos of what they ate for lunch.

Pages 6–7: Eating Together

Ask children to draw a picture of their lunch table, and help them to write the names of who sits where. They can add images of what they like eating best for lunch and appropriate cutlery in the right places. Discuss table manners and allow children to practice asking for things.

Pages 8–9: Sandwiches

Make pretend sandwiches using thin colored foam or painted cardboard for the bread and ingredients. You could role-play a sandwich "bar." Ask children to sort the ingredients into different containers. Two children can play servers, assembling sandwiches to order. The others can be customers, lining up, choosing, ordering, and paying for their lunches.

Pages 10–11: Lunch at Home

The photograph on the page shows a Japanese family using chopsticks. Provide the children with chopsticks and small pieces of food, such as raisins, to pick up and eat.

Pages 12–13: Hot and Cold

Grow a salad ingredient together. Cress is simplest and can be grown in yogurt tubs on a sunny windowsill at any time of the year. However, if you have the space available and it's the right season, why not grow tomatoes in bags or pots? Cherry tomatoes are especially appealing to young children.

Pages 14–15: Lunch Outside

Teach the children the words and music to the "Teddy bears' picnic" – if they don't know it already. Then organize a pretend teddy bears' picnic using plastic plates and cups, and pretend foods (plastic, wood, or homemade from salt dough).

Pages 16–17: Something Sweet

Make some fruity jigsaw puzzles. Find big photos of fruit, stick on to cardboard for strength, and then cut up to make jigsaw pieces.

Pages 18–19: Lunchtime Drinks

Provide a plastic pitcher of water and containers so children can practice pouring. Turn this into a musical activity for older children by using glass beakers, filled with different amounts of water. Children can tap the side of each glass gently with a wooden spoon to produce notes of different pitches.

Pages 20–21: Make It: Greek Salad

Organize a blind tasting of different salad ingredients, such as tomatoes, cucumber, lettuce, radish, celery, sweet peppers, avocado, and grated carrot. See which ones children can identify.

Index

b
bananas **16, 17**
barbecued food **14**
bread **21**

c
chopsticks **10**

d
drinks **18–19**
dumplings **15**

f
family lunches **10–11**
fruit **16**

m
milkshakes **19**

p
pita **21**

s
salads **13, 20–21**
sandwiches **8, 9**
sausages **9**
school lunches **6–7**
smoothies **19**
soup **12**

Picture acknowledgments:
Alamy: 6-7 (Rob Wilkinson), 12 (Real World People), 15 (Tina Manley), 20-21 (© Profimedia International s.r.o.); **Corbis:** cover tablecloth, 2-3, 22-24 (Gregor Schuster), 10-11 (Redlink), 18 (Sean Justice); **Evans:** 9 (Gareth Boden); **Getty:** cover (StockFood Creative), 4-5 (Vanessa Davies), 13 (Peter Dazeley/The Image Bank), 16 (Anne Ackermann); **iStockphoto:** cover sky (Judy Foldetta), 17, 19 (Olga Lyubkina); **Photolibrary:** 8 (Pacific Stock), 14 (Foodpix).

With special thanks to Nicky and Luke Parker for the use of the photograph on page 9.

24